WhY were hen toes like that...?

and other
SHORT STORIES

Illustrations by: Shanny Farrow, age 12, Coteland's School, Jade Cooper, age 10, Five Oaks Middle School, Olivia Gillespie age 9, Caroline Logan, age 10, Stenton Primary School

Why were her toes like that...?

and other
SHORT STORIES

An anthology of winning stories from the 2007
World Book Day story writing competition

www.evansbooks.co.uk

www.worldbookday.com
Sponsored by National Book Tokens

Published in 2008 by Evans Brothers Limited
2A Portman Mansions
Chiltern Street
London WIU 6NR

British Library Cataloguing in Publication Data
A catalogue record for this book is available from the
British Library

ISBN: 9780237536107

Editor: Su Swallow
Designer: Rebecca Fox

Foreword

What talent! I have just finished reading dozens and dozens of splendid stories by youngsters aged 6-16 from all over the British Isles – and I am flabbergasted at the range, subtlety and imagination of their work.

Before going any further, therefore, I wish to offer my most sincere congratulations to all 3,000 students who joined in this year's Evans/World Book Day short story bonanza. The number of entrants far exceeded expectation and the standard of creativity and literary awareness was universally high. I only wish we could have printed all the stories received.

Unfortunately this was not possible. Instead, Evans' editors selected a shortlist of sixty stories. From this list I had the unenviable task of choosing just a dozen for printing, two beginning with each of the six opening lines.

The stories that follow are not necessarily the 'best' – how could one possibly compare a story written by a six-year-old with one written by a teenager? – but a cross-section of the most imaginative, well-constructed, original and thoughtful pieces from all age-groups and geographical areas (including France!).

Apart from ensuring a representative selection, I based my choice on these criteria: (1) sticking to the rules (one fine story was ruled out because the author changed the words of the opening); (2) originality (try not to write the first thing that comes into your head because it will probably be similar to something you have read or seen recently); (3) exciting language (it's a good idea to avoid expressions you are used to seeing in print); (4) craft (I like well-punctuated stories with a shape!).

As I was reading through the stories a second time, my daughter Ellie asked which one I liked best. I chose Madeleine Latham's. Do you agree? Whether you do or not, I'm sure you'll share my delight in every one of the twelve gems that follow.

Stewart Ross
Blean
December 2007

Acknowledgments

We would like to thank every single student who contributed to the 3,000 entries we received. We really enjoyed reading the huge mixture of stories, which ranged from portals to other worlds, time travel, weird and wacky aliens, new-found relatives and bizarre magical afflictions!

We would also like to thank all the teachers and librarians who took the trouble to enter their schools and made the effort to ensure that the first World Book Day/Evans Short Story Competition was so successful. If you didn't win this year, please don't be discouraged from entering in the future!

We owe a huge "thank you" to the six authors for contributing their first lines: Caroline Lawrence, Charlie Higson, Dame Jacqueline Wilson, Malorie Blackman, Michael Rosen and in particular to Stewart Ross for the time and effort he put into the difficult process of judging the competition.

And last but not least, thank you to Cathy Schofield from World Book Day and Truda Spruyt at Colman Getty for all their help in making the competition happen.

Log onto **www.worldbookday.com** or **www.evansbooks.co.uk** for information on next year's competition.

contents

Arran knew that he should be scared. If he was watching this on television, he would be hiding behind the sofa right now, so why was he calmly standing there while this whole terrible scene unfolded around him?

Charlie Higson

Deceivers: Trust No One

Alistair Godley, age 14,
South Axholme Community School, Doncaster

Arran knew that he should be scared. If he was watching this on television, he would be hiding behind the sofa right now, so why was he calmly standing there while this whole terrible scene unfolded around him?

The green velvet pouch lay innocently on the old, oak coffee table of Arran's front room. At its neck, the cotton green cord, tied tightly and precisely with a knot, concealed the contents within. He leant forward, stretching out his arm, in an attempt to pick up the object in front of him. He couldn't do it. He had craved it for so long. Now, it was his. He retreated his arm; he would take a quick glance later.

A smirk slid across his face – it had been much easier than expected...

It was the dead of a bitter cold night in Filbert Street, and the only noise to be heard was the hoot of an owl as it nurtured its young. No movement. Until, that is, the door to number 9 opened and closed without even a creak. A man of around 20 stood on the front step. He looked up at the indigo sea of stars, twinkling like Christmas lights. He looked straight ahead once more and began to glide down the steps and along the pavement which ran adjacent to the odd-numbered houses. Suddenly, there was a rustle in the coniferous bushes on the opposite side of the road. Arran stopped moving, and turned. 'You can come out now,' he said loudly.

He had no sympathy for any neighbour who might still be living in the street, and who would most likely be sleeping at this unearthly hour. A dark figure emerged from the jungle of plants, rising up above Arran's head. He stepped closer and closer towards him. 'Glad you could make it, JD,' spoke Arran confidently.

'You speak as if you cannot trust me,' he

replied. 'You know I wish to take a back seat now.'

'You speak as if you cannot trust me, *sir*.'

'Sorry. You speak as if you cannot trust me, sir.'

'That's better. Well, we'll have to see how you fair tonight, eh JD?'

'Yes.' There was a slight cough by Arran. 'Yes, sir.'

'Good. You're learning. Well, that's enough chat. We can't stand here all night, we've got places to be.'

Immediately, the two of them set off at a brisk pace, continuing along the pavement until they reached the junction at the main road. With ease, they crossed – there was little traffic at such a time – turned left and began marching up Carbon Lane, that led to the centre of the city.

Once they reached the junction, the two men dived into the shadows and began cautiously moving towards the final destination. Past the bank and past the estate agents. They were the first places he was going after tonight.

There it was. Standing tall, proud, yet elegant under the twilight. The Carbon Museum. Built out of limestone more than 50 years ago, pollution and acidic precipitation had dissolved the outer layer of rock. The gargoyles of the main entrance no longer had distinguishable features – a round block of rock. In the daytime, the building was swarming with security staff, but now, oddly, there were none to be seen. Stage 1 complete, Stage 2 beginning…

Arran and JD scrambled across the road as fast as they could and threw themselves flat against the side wall. Arran looked up; the CCTV camera was pointing the other way. Lucky. He looked up in the other direction, seeing the open window on the fourth floor, whilst JD scanned the area, keeping watch for any passer-by. No one knew his real name. In fact, 'JD' was all they knew, along with the fact that he did not stay in one place for long – he was France's most wanted burglar.

'Are we clear?' Arran asked sharply.

'Yeh.'

'Give me a leg up then,' he commanded.

JD sighed and shook his head before bending down and presenting his hands in a cup position. Arran placed his muddy trainer onto his accomplice's hands. 'Mustn't forget these,' he whispered, displaying a pair of the finest leather gloves. He slipped them onto his stubby hands. He felt the smooth, soft leather caress his skin. Only the best will do. He put his weight onto his right foot which remained in JD's hand. He sprang upwards and clung on to the drainpipe as if his life depended on it. He blew unsteadily in the sudden gust of wind, until it dropped and he was still once more. Gently, Arran placed both feet on the pipe and began to clamber slowly upwards, minding not to stay in one place too long, should the pipe not be strong enough.

He reached the open window, knowing exactly where it led. Sliding onto the ledge, he clicked his fingers twice. The sound reverberated around the street, but JD knew what it meant, that was the signal. Scanning the area for the last time, he leapt onto the drainpipe and shimmied himself upwards, until he reached Arran. The two of them climbed in, as silent as the owl flies. However, they remained on the inside windowsill – the floor was carpeted with red lasers. That was the least of their worries though.

The laser problem was easily overcome. The power box was situated on the opposite wall in the corner. Arran took a metal object from his pocket. A bullet. He hurtled it at the black box. There was a spark as the electrical supply was lost and the lasers disappeared. Both of them leapt onto the floor, jumped up and sprinted to the main exhibit entrance.

Glistening in the centre of the room, like a star in the night sky, was the diamond. 'Le plus grand diamant' was its name, meaning 'the biggest diamond'. Abruptly, a door creaked open on the other side of the room, and in stepped the security guard in charge of the diamond's protection. Arran and JD remained unseen in the shadows. The security chief stepped towards the showcase. There was no security system on the diamond, now that the museum had closed, and because he had come to take the jewel to the safe overnight, until the museum re-opened at 6:00am the following morning. He dropped it into a green, velvet pouch, and placed it in his coat pocket.

This was expected by the two intruders though. Arran slipped his hand into his black corduroy trouser pocket and pulled out a pistol with a silencer on the end. He aimed it at the head of the security guard, who was walking back towards the door he had entered by.

The light left the protector's eyes. He fell in one motion to the floor. Thud!

'Go,' commanded Arran in a whispered voice.

JD glided across the room to the body of the security guard, with his back facing Arran. Slowly and conspicuously, he slipped his hand into his pocket and produced something. He delved his hand into the dead man's pocket and pulled out the green velvet pouch. He placed something in his own pocket and glided back to Arran, who still had the gun, holding it close to his chest. 'Here you are, sir.'

Arran took the green velvet pouch, before pointing the gun at JD. 'Thanks.'

Before Arran could pull the trigger, JD had kicked the gun out of his hand. It flew across the room and landed in the shadow of the mining exhibit. JD darted back down the main corridor, leapt out of the window, and ran off down the street, eventually disappearing from sight.

Arran, still squatting in the shadows, was frozen. Stunned. He had the diamond though. He no longer needed JD anyway. Now he wouldn't need paying either. Perfect. He followed in the footsteps of his accomplice and disappeared from view.

Now, there it was. Lying delicately on the tabletop of Arran's living room. He could no longer contain his excitement, so snatched the pouch off the table, produced a knife, and cut the green cotton cord. However, there was no glistening in the light; no sparkling star.

Arran placed his trembling hand inside the pouch, pulling out the object. A marble. 'Aaaargh!' he bellowed.

The scream penetrated the ears of neighbours and was heard by the entire town, including the squatter of a dilapidated, terraced house on the outskirts, where a man holding a green, velvet pouch was laughing hysterically, holding a star.

COULROPHOBIA

Ross Howard, age 12,
Castle View School, Essex

Arran knew that he should be scared. If he was watching this on television, he would be hiding behind the sofa right now, so why was he calmly standing there while this whole terrible scene unfolded around him? As he stood transfixed, he thought back to how he got into this horrific situation.

Arran had always hated clowns. Always. So when his eccentric teacher Mrs Lefty revealed to the class that the end-of-year trip was to the circus that very afternoon, and everyone's parents had already been notified, Arran was furious. Everyone in class knew that Arran despised clowns but not only was he angry at his teacher, he was angry at his parents for not remembering to tell Mrs Lefty.

Later, as they bumped along on the school bus, Arran stared out of the window, a sick feeling in his gut. Something bad was going to happen, his mind told him. *Oh, shut up, wussy,* he said to himself. *This is the perfect opportunity to overcome my fear.* But as the bus drove steadily on, he felt increasingly anxious.

By the time he'd bought himself some popcorn, a drink and had sat down in the hard, plastic chairs, Arran was trying to stop himself from shaking. His best friend Ernie, who had noticed this, nudged him in the arm.

'You'll be alright mate!' he said, licking fluffy candyfloss from one of his pudgy fingers. Arran just smiled nervously and turned to face the ring.

After the first few minutes, Arran really began to enjoy himself. He gaped as Marcello the Magician pulled a fifth white rabbit out of his hat, and awed as the Monkey Men swung through the ring on ropes and began performing cartwheels and somersaults. It was when the clowns finally came driving in that the horror began.

Arran stood up and was about to walk out when Ernie sat him back down again. 'It's alright,' he said, bursting out laughing as two clowns put a custard pie into each other's faces. One clown, driving along in a small car, leapt in the air, performed a somersault and landed on the ringside doing a handstand. He sprang back onto his feet and turned his face to the audience. A stretching smile and big blue eyes pierced Arran's vision. He reeled back in fear. He jumped up but this time, when Ernie tried to sit him back down again, he simply shoved his huge arm off and stormed away.

Ernie rushed up to Arran outside. 'I'm sorry Ernie,' Arran began. 'I just can't do it!'

'It's alright,' his friend replied. 'I shouldn't have...' He paused.

A weird noise was emanating from inside the Big Top tent. They looked at each other in confusion as they dashed inside to see the audience clutching their heads and screaming in agony. All of the clowns were standing in the ring cackling. Arran gasped. Waves of what seemed to be some sort of energy were shooting from the audience's heads and being absorbed into the clowns' evil, grimacing faces.

Arran shook uncontrollably, jolting himself back to the present scene. He turned to run, only to find two scary-looking clowns blocking his path; one holding an unconscious Ernie.

'Sweet dreams,' the other said and then the club descended and Arran was out cold.

Arran opened his eyes to see the leering face of the clown who had been driving the car staring into his eyes. 'Peekaboo!' it giggled.

Arran tried to run away but was gripped tightly by the huge clown who had knocked him out. He looked to the side of him. Ernie was semi-conscious in the grip of another big clown. 'Wh-who are you?' Arran stammered.

'You might call us clowns,' the leader said, 'but our proper names are Xenoclownictophoyders. We are aliens from a different planet, different universe. Our own planet was destroyed many years ago by beings from another galaxy. Thankfully, we managed to escape before the disaster and for a while we travelled in space with no home and nowhere to go... then we found Earth.

Our people have been coming to Earth for

years in spaceships appearing to you as circus tents.' He pointed around him. 'Your people found our appearance rather amusing so we created 'The Circus' and shortened our names to 'clowns'. This candyfloss machine you see in front of you drains information from your brains and absorbs it into our own. Each time we do this, we become more human. Once complete we can invite the rest of our race to this planet and take it over for ourselves. When we have drained your brains and wiped your memories, we will begin our reign of supremacy!'

Suddenly, Ernie burst into tears. 'Please don't kill us!' he pleaded.

A pained expression appeared on the faces of the clowns as they too burst into tears and their bodies began to shake.

'You can't stand sadness, can you?' Arran asked in surprise. 'You like bringing joy to people. It's part of your nature.'

'Well, we are clowns,' the leader wept.

'Listen, let's make a deal,' Arran said anxiously. 'You take your information from us, wipe our memories and become human. Don't destroy us or you'll be no better than those who destroyed your planet. You can stay in your circus, bring your others here and live amongst us bringing fun and laughter to people.'

There were a few moments of silence as the clowns pondered their situation. Then a huge grin spread across the face of the leader. 'It's a deal!' he nodded, grasping Arran's hand with his large white glove. He reached for the candyfloss machine aiming it at Arran and Ernie. There was an eerie sound, a flash of light and then nothing.

The next Saturday of the holidays, Arran walked into the kitchen where his mum, dad and younger brother James sat around the table. 'Listen,' his mum said, 'I hope you don't mind but we've bought tickets for the circus. I forgot about your phobia and if you don't want to go, we can cancel it if you want.'

'No, it's OK,' Arran replied. 'I'd love to go!' and he smiled. Did he remember after all?

I opened my front door and then gasped, gazing into the house in total astonishment.

Jacqueline Wilson

Anna

Emily Waldron, age 11,
British Section - Collège les Hauts Grillets à Sections Internationales,
France

I opened my front door and then gasped, gazing into the house in total astonishment. My parents were in front of the fireplace with a little girl between them. She looked about 6 years old, had brown hair, brown eyes and sallow skin. Who was she? I don't have a sister or much in the way of family. My parents told me that Dad found her while cutting up logs in the mountains. You don't find orphans in the mountains – it's too cold and they get eaten by cougars. We asked her her name, what she was doing up there, and she refused to answer. She seemed to understand us – perhaps she was too exhausted to talk.

My parents decided that it would be better

if she stayed with us overnight, as it was already getting dark and the paths down the mountains are not safe at night.

Next morning, over breakfast, she told us that she came from the mountains of Zashula, high in the Eastern range.

'How did you get over to us, little one?' asked my father.

'I found a donkey and he took me some of the way. After he died I walked,' she said.

'All on your own?' I asked.

'I decided to keep going on,' she murmured, 'as I did not want to die alone up in the mountains.' She told us that she was an orphan; that her parents had died after their house had been destroyed by rebels. On her way back from school she saw the whole village in flames and realised that she could never go back.

My mother felt sorry for her. Her whole family was dead and she would be at risk from the rebels if they tracked her down. My father said that if the rebels found her they would find anyone who had helped her and kill them too. 'There's only one solution,' said my mother. 'We will keep her and she will become our daughter.'

I didn't mind – it was boring all on my own, particularly when the snow came down and we were trapped in the house for weeks. It would be nice to have someone to play with. We were well off and could afford another mouth to feed. One mystery remained. What was her name? She refused to tell us and so we called her Anna.

Two years passed, and we told her everything we knew. Her customs were different from ours, her accent was strange, and she needed to fit in. She learned to talk like us and how to behave. One thing we couldn't change was the way she looked. I am tall and blonde and so are my people. She looked nothing like us. Outsiders would never believe that she was part of our family. My parents decided that it was too risky for her to go to school, so they taught her themselves – simple lessons and stories about the mountains. Her favourite was the story of Father Christmas. She would ask us to tell again and again how he flew through the sky with his reindeer and sledge, bringing presents to good children. 'Have I been good?' she would ask. 'Will I get a present? Can he bring my parents back?'

At Christmas she decided to stay up and

wait for Father Christmas. On Christmas night I was sleeping and a strange sound disturbed me. I woke up immediately. My room was small and panelled in wood. The shutters were closed. I could smell wood smoke from the fire and a strange smell that I had never smelled before. Far across the valley I heard the church bell peeling midnight. I swung my legs out of bed. It was cold – the wooden floor was freezing. I went down to the kitchen and saw that the back door was open. Snow was falling hard, and as I crossed into the cold, dark iciness that was outside, I saw a figure. It was Anna. She was standing bare-legged in the snow with a guttering candle in her hand. I cried out to her and tried to run over to her but suddenly there was a blinding blue flash that flung me against the wall. After that I do not remember anything.

The next day my parents found me out cold in a heap next to the wall. Anna had disappeared. We called out search parties. Men from the village, who knew Father well, were trustworthy, and expert trackers came and searched. We didn't put up posters or tell other villages – it was too risky. Even after they gave up, my father kept looking.

He spent all day out in the cold, climbing into the high peaks hoping for a glimpse of her or a clue as to what had become of her. After four months we had to give up. We were desolate. I missed Anna more than I could say.

When spring came, when the snows melted and the flowers started to bloom, we found her body, next to the river. She was buried next to the pine tree – she had loved to climb it.

Another year passed. It was Christmas again. Once again I was woken by a strange sound outside. I went down the stairs cautiously this time. I opened the kitchen door and saw Anna in the shimmering snow. Delicate snowflakes were drifting down. I was sure it was Anna – but she looked cold and pale. I tried to touch her but my hand went right through her.

'I came back,' she said.

'Why?' I asked.

'To tell you what you always wanted to know,' she replied. 'My name. I am called Anoushka, and you would have recognised my name because my father was the chief of our people. The rebels killed him for our land and our gold. The Eastern Mountains are full of precious gems, hidden by my people, and the rebels want them. If they had found me they would have killed us all. Tell your parents, but no one else. Farewell.'

'Wait,' I cried. 'Don't go!' There was something more important that I wanted to know. 'Did you see Father Christmas?' I asked.

'Oh yes,' she replied, 'and he has given me my parents back.'

Ghost-Like

Rumour Giles, age 13,
Barton Court Grammar School, Kent

I opened my front door and then gasped,
gazing into the house in total astonishment.
Two police officers were sitting on the sofa;
my mum was crying into my dad's shoulder, my
older sister Gabrielle was staring into space with
tears streaming. I ran to them and asked what had
happened, they didn't even look at me. I shouted
right in their faces but it was like I was invisible.
I gave up and sat down on the floor, my heart
beating as fast as if I'd been sprinting. The small,
blonde policewoman was saying something about
someone shooting a girl, a gun and DNA samples.
I started to get an uneasy feeling in my stomach. It
was then that she said the girl's name.

It was mine. Lily.

I stayed sitting on the floor for hours after the police left, my legs were too weak to move, and I felt dizzy. How could I be dead? If I was dead, why could I still feel things like hunger and fear? Gabrielle came back into the room and sat on the sofa. She buried her head in her arms and knees, her long blonde hair covering her face; we were very close sisters, we never argued except over silly things like the hair straighteners or the TV remote. I reached out and tried to put my arms around her. It was strange, I could feel her but it was like I had pins and needles whenever I touched her. She looked up suddenly, looking startled, and went into the kitchen. Tears welled up in my eyes, but though I cried they just disappeared into nowhere. I curled up on the floor and drifted into a strange sleep.

The next morning, I left the house and walked along to my old school. There were police officers around the gates, and people taking photos and everything. It was very weird, all the girls from the school were whispering about what had happened all day. Apparently I'd been just walking out of the school gates with my friends and a shot had come out of nowhere; my best friend Gina was surrounded by a cluster of girls at break and lunch clucking round her like hens. I tried to hug her like I hugged Gabrielle and she shivered. I'd only ever seen Gina cry once before, when she was in nursery school with me and a boy pushed her out of the way to go on the slide first. That's how long we'd been friends. I hated seeing her pretty face all pale and sad. Gina had always been the pretty one, with bright-green eyes and dark-brown hair all down her back, but I'd been more friendly and confident. I followed her around the school for a while and eventually went home, not quite knowing what was going on. *So this is how it feels to be a ghost*, I thought. I wondered if I'd have to stay like this forever, or if I'd go to Heaven, but I had no idea what I had to do to go to Heaven. I pushed the scary thoughts from my mind and concentrated on the ones I loved.

The next day my story was on the news; a picture of me hung up behind a serious-looking woman. It went on to say that *another* girl had been shot in the exact same place a few hours ago. I was really shocked, as the girl had looked quite similar to me and like I said had been killed in the exact same place. I'd never talked to her before, but I knew her name was Grace. The police turned up and told us this case was getting really serious now, they had no idea who the killer was but the pattern of victims seemed to be teenage blonde girls. I got very upset and cried non-existent tears again. I didn't want any more families to have to go through what mine and Grace's were; it was awful watching helplessly as my mum started smoking more and more and cried all the time, seeing my sister sleep in a room and touch every single one of my things before going to bed. My dad was keeping his grief under control, doing everything he could to help the police, but I could see his pain when he sat in front of the TV in the dark watching the programmes we loved and doing the crossword that we always did together.

That night, I struggled very hard with my thoughts and feelings. I tried to force my head into remembering the killer's face; I sat for hours until my head ached. I was just about to drift off when I suddenly saw the killer in my mind as clear as glass: it had been a middle-aged woman, no one could ever suspect her. She had wild, curly brown hair and big shadows under her eyes, her skin was tired and she looked quite mad, her bright blue eyes bulging. I raced down to the police station, wondering how on earth I could tell them who had killed Grace and me. I spotted a tube of bright red lipstick and desperately scribbled on the window:

This isn't a trick. Mrs Matthews from 12 Bate Lane killed Lily and Grace. Investigate her.

I waited anxiously around the station all night. I had been pacing around and my legs felt stiff but I didn't care. Eventually a cleaner came into the office I was in and gasped when he read the message. He sounded the alarm and the police in charge of my case were talking very fast and not stopping. I gave a silent cry of frustration when they discussed it as maybe a false statement, but they agreed to investigate Mrs Matthews in the end.

I followed them eagerly to her house, a bleak council house with boarded-up windows and very filthy. As soon as she opened the door Mrs Matthews burst into tears and admitted everything; she was arrested and taken away. The police were still baffled as to who left the message but I ran straight through the doors where Mrs Matthews was being questioned and listened too. After all, I thought I had the right.

Apparently Mrs Matthews had had a blonde teenage daughter exactly like Grace and me; her daughter had suffered from very serious anorexia nervosa and had collapsed with heart failure. When she'd seen me she thought she was seeing her daughter and also the next day thought Grace had been a ghost of her daughter as well. She went to prison and I was left sitting invisibly in the small square room; I was suddenly filled with a great mix of feelings. My family had been called and assured that the killer had been found, Mrs Matthews was taken, and after her prison sentence was to be admitted to a mental hospital for mothers who'd lost their children. But best of all, somehow in my unbeating heart, I'd managed to forgive her. I was just glad that it was over and then a great silver beam of light suddenly opened up above my head. It reflected off my face making my eyes squint at the brightness. *Am I going to Heaven?* I asked myself. The light shone on my long blonde hair, and I was then immersed in it.

I opened my eyes. They were big and blue and staring. My mum and dad, Gabrielle and Gina were all sitting round me. I was propped up on a white linen bed. They were all smiling and looked the happiest ever; this was the most confused I'd ever been. Gabrielle leaned over and took my hand. 'You've been in a coma, a short one, but we thought we'd lost you! You were shot but the police have found the criminal.'

I couldn't say anything; I just grasped all their hands in mine and closed my eyes tight. I hadn't really been dead, it was probably just my spirit, the police had never actually said I was dead, I'd just assumed so.

I kept my ghost-like secret to myself all my life; it was too strange for anyone to comprehend. But from then on, Grace was a great friend; she was the only one who'd had the same experience. I'll just say I appreciated life much more afterwards.

'No you can't,' growled Uncle Turpin, without even looking up from his dinner.

Stewart Ross

How Aunt Iris Gets Fat

Hazel Minty, age 6,
Chestnut Lane Infant School, Buckinghamshire

'**No you can't,' growled Uncle Turpin, without even looking up from his dinner.** Aunt Iris had just asked Uncle Turpin for some ketchup for her spaghetti but Uncle Turpin wanted it all for himself because he was fat and mean. Aunt Iris asked that because they were in their messy, smelly kitchen. The floor was sticky and covered with old rotting food. There was a huge untidy pile of dirty dishes and cups and saucers in the sink. Aunt Iris and Uncle Turpin were rubbish at washing up.

'That's not fair!' shouted Aunt Iris. She really wanted some ketchup.

So the next day Aunt Iris woke up early,

sneaked downstairs into the kitchen and put dyed worms with earwax into the ketchup. She got some worms from the garden and put red dye on them. They wriggled through some earwax and it was sticky so it stuck to them. Then they wriggled into the ketchup bottle. Next she got some more worms from the garden, mushed them up in the grinder and put them in the ketchup bottle. Then Aunt Iris put the lid on the ketchup bottle and shook it around to mix it all up.

That night Aunt Iris made dauphinoise potatoes for tea and grizzly Uncle Turpin squirted all the ketchup on his plate. Then he tasted it and said, 'UUUURRRSSHHHH!!' He coughed like mad and was sick all over the kitchen. Now the kitchen was in a real mess and the floor was even stickier.

'Is something the matter?' asked Aunt Iris. She was trying to sound sweet and smiling as if she really cared about Uncle Turpin.

'This is disgusting,' shouted Uncle Turpin. 'I'm never ever, ever having dauphinoise potatoes again.' Aunt Iris smiled a secret smile and started to laugh. Her shoulders were shaking and her tummy was bumping up and down. Aunt Iris tried to stop but she couldn't. It was so funny that Uncle Turpin thought it was the potatoes that tasted weird and not the ketchup. Aunt Iris put her hand over her mouth to stop herself laughing and the laugh would not stop. She held her hand over her mouth so much that she started to cough. She coughed like mad and then she was sick all over the kitchen. What a mess!!

'Oh my dear,' said Uncle Turpin. 'The dauphinoise potatoes have made you sick too. They are so disgusting you must never ever, ever make them again.'

'OK then,' said Aunt Iris. They had to tidy up the kitchen that night.

So the next day Aunt Iris got another bottle of ketchup and decided she would make it taste even more disgusting than the first bottle. She got some more worms from the garden and did the same as she did before. The worms wriggled through earwax, they wriggled across a bar of red soap, they wriggled through some dead bugs and they wriggled through red toothpaste. Next they wriggled into the ketchup bottle and Aunt Iris put the lid on and shook it around to mix it all up.

That night Aunt Iris made plain potatoes

for tea and grizzly Uncle Turpin squirted all the ketchup on the plain potatoes. Then he tasted it and said, 'UUURRSSHH!!!!!!!' again. 'This is disgusting,' shouted Uncle Turpin. 'I'm never ever, ever having plain potatoes again.'

Aunt Iris smiled a secret smile again and started to laugh. BUT this time Uncle Turpin saw her laughing. 'Is it the ketchup?' asked Uncle Turpin.

Aunt Iris said, 'Yes. Perhaps you shouldn't eat ketchup any more if you think it's so disgusting. I will never ever, ever give you ketchup again my dear.'

From then on Aunt Iris always had the ketchup all to herself and got fatter and fatter every day until she was as fat as Uncle Turpin.

An Easter Story

Madeleine Latham, age 11,
Oxford High School, Oxford

'**No you can't!' growled Uncle Turpin, without even looking up from his dinner.** Marvellous. We had been stuck here for the last three weeks and we were beginning to wonder whether he was actually capable of saying the magic word 'Yes' or even, Heaven forbid, 'What a good idea.'

Uncle Turpin wasn't really our uncle. He wasn't related to us at all. He was our parents' lawyer and, in what can only have been a moment of complete insanity, they had appointed him as our guardian while they went off on yet another trip to study the nesting habits of blue macaws in deepest, darkest Brazil. Uncle Turpin didn't have any children of his own, or even a wife come to think of it, and knew as much about children as we did about Einstein's theory of relativity. To say we were all looking forward to our parents coming home was putting it mildly.

Anyway, what I had actually asked him was if it would be okay if we buried our little brother, Aloysius, in the orchard. It was almost Easter and we had learned all about Christ rising from the dead in RS and we were quite keen to give it a go. When I say we, I mean me, my twin sister Camilla and my brothers Hector and Oliver. Aloysius was almost six years old and was definitely the most annoying six-year-old on the planet, which is why he had been selected, very democratically of course. We weren't intending burying him completely. We were thinking more along the lines of up to his neck. Anyway Uncle Turpin had said 'No you can't,' in that 'Don't even think about it' sort of voice, so it was back to square one.

But just when we were about to give up and think of another way of whiling away the school holiday, we had a stroke of luck. Hector had been in the garden, trying to hit pigeons with his catapult, when he spotted a blackbird that had got all tangled up in the net on the tennis court and it looked pretty dead to us. We had a vote and all agreed the blackbird could substitute for Aloysius and set about digging the hole. We wrapped the bird in one of Uncle Turpin's shirts that we sneaked off the washing line and carefully laid it in the hole and covered it over with earth. We had a sort of funeral from the bits we remembered from when our grandmother died and crossed our fingers for luck.

We were desperate to know what was going to happen and having to wait for three days to find out was unbearable. The most important thing was making sure Uncle Turpin (aka Spoilsport) didn't find out what we were up to and Hector and Oliver made it perfectly clear to Aloysius what they would do to him if he let the cat out of the bag. But anyway, he was so grateful it wasn't him in that hole that he would have gone along with anything. The time dragged on and by the next morning we couldn't contain ourselves any longer. So we went and had a little peek. The blackbird was still there! Camilla, as usual, almost ruined everything by saying she thought only the soul went to Heaven so how would we be able to tell if anything had happened, but Oliver managed to find a picture in one of his Bible-stories books definitely showing Jesus alive again and we all relaxed.

Two days to go and by now the anticipation was killing us. And that's when it happened. They arrived. Mum and Dad. From Brazil. To take us home. No more of Uncle Turpin's cooking. In fact, no more of Uncle Turpin. We were beside ourselves with happiness and excitement. We packed in about fifteen minutes flat and before we knew it, we were in the car, waving goodbye to Uncle Turpin and heading for the motorway, all talking at a hundred miles an hour. And then we remembered. THE BLACKBIRD. We could hardly confess, could we, and so, to this day almost thirty years later, we still don't know. Do you?

'You must never
open it,' said
my brother.
'Promise me you'll
never open it.'

Malorie Blackman

The Magical Box

Jade Longley, age 9,
The Study Preparatory School, London

'You must never open it,' said my brother. 'Promise me you'll never open it.'

'I promise, but why won't you tell me what lies inside?'

'You may only open it on your seventeenth birthday,' my brother told me mysteriously.

Our mother died when my brother and I were very young, and our grandmother had been given the responsibility of taking care of us. My brother, as the elder sibling, had been entrusted with handing down the secret box. This box had been passed down from generation to generation in our family, each time the older brother or sister guarding its secrecy until the younger child would be old enough to watch over it.

The box was small enough to hold between two cupped hands. Parts of the box showed signs of age – an emerald stone was missing from a circle of jewels on the lid of the box, although its setting still remained. One corner had been flattened; it had probably been knocked many years ago. As a result, the gold paint had been chipped, revealing the dull brown of the wood underneath. The only part of the box that remained unblemished was the pure-gold lock that held the lid securely closed, and in this way the contents were kept hidden from the outside world.

'At dusk on your seventeenth birthday you must remember to turn the key of the box. At no other time can it be opened,' explained my brother.

'But please, please won't you tell me what's inside?' I asked impatiently.

'That is something I cannot answer. You will have to wait and see.'

Years passed, and every birthday I would create a different scene in my mind of what might lie inside the delicate little box. I ran my fingers over the velvety cover; I smelled the dusty stitching along the sides of the box. Each time I fought against the urge to open it.

At last the night before my seventeenth birthday arrived. I tossed and turned in my bed, unable to sleep.

Morning came, but dusk seemed so far away. I opened all my presents and enjoyed a birthday supper of my grandmother's homemade steak pie. My brother and grandmother mentioned nothing about the box for the whole of that day. I am sure they suspected how curious I must be, but perhaps they were waiting to see if I would remember. I was too nervous and excited to discuss it with them.

I peered through a crack in the curtains and I could see that the sky was darkening. The time had come. I left the sitting room quietly and the only words I spoke were, 'I shall do it now.' My grandmother nodded in her warm and affectionate way as I went through the door. I climbed the narrow staircase to the attic. There was the box waiting for me on the top shelf of the bookcase. Trembling, I crossed the room. My fingers quivered as I fumbled for the lock.

As I opened the box, I felt a soft breeze on

my cheeks. The musty smell of my grandmother's attic disappeared and instead I smelt fresh flowers. I felt myself growing smaller and smaller and grabbed hold of something rough, maybe the branch of a tree, as I was swept inside the box.

I stood gazing in amazement at a shimmering pool of water. The surface of the water shone like a mirror, catching the reflection of the beautiful flowers and trees surrounding the lake. As I looked closer I could see the faint outline of fairylike creatures. I recognised them as water sylphs from a story I had once read. They were dressed from head to toe in blue, all different shades of blue.

They spoke in a language I could not understand. Even though I was standing above them, they did not seem to notice me. I gazed at them intently for a few moments. They danced in and out of the shadows. It seemed to me that there were six of them altogether. I tore my eyes away from them to look at the rest of the garden.

Sweet tulips stood in rows at either side of the path. Willows gently brushed the surface of the water. I could hear the sounds of birds singing in the night sky. I desperately wanted to take something home with me to remind me of this beautiful place. I noticed a fallen rose at the edge of the lake, and gently lifted it up. The rose was yellow with fiery orange tips. I placed the rose in the folds of my long skirt and rushed happily around the garden, somehow knowing that I would never have the luck to visit this special place again. Then I realised that the flowers and trees around me were starting to wither and the colours started to quickly drain out of everything. The flowers lost their perfume and the rich blues of the night turned to an empty grey.

A distant voice murmured, 'Put it back, put it back, or our world will die.'

I realised that I had taken something that did not belong to me; I had stolen something from their world. I let the flower fall from my skirt. As I let go, a sylph rose from the centre of the lake and whispered, 'Thank you. You have kept to our rules. We know we can trust you. You may return here every year on your birthday until you die. Every person in your family so far has been allowed to return here. Go back now for it is late, but keep our secret safe. See you next year. Farewell!'

I gasped and whispered, 'But how do I get back to my world?'

'Goodbye!' the sylph said softly and disappeared without a sound under the clear water.

A breeze swept me off my feet and I returned to the attic. There was a quiet thud as the lid of the magical box closed. My secret would rest on the old bookshelf until next year.

Times Two

Gareth McNamara, age 14,
Scoil Damhnait, Ireland

Y ou must never open it,' said my brother.
'Promise me you'll never open it.'
I looked into his serious blue eyes, almost
identical to mine, the only common feature that
hinted we were related. There was something
in those eyes, something urgent and fearful,
something I couldn't refuse. I nodded solemnly.

Three days later, Alexis was dead.

My name's Haze. Hazel Wolfram Cain. A feminine
sounding tree, a German boy's name and Adam
and Eve's murderous son. I will never understand
just what my parents were thinking when they
named me.

I like to think of myself as a fairly trustworthy person. After Alexis died, I kept my word. I didn't think the fact he'd never be able to find out if I broke my promise made a difference. The battered old jewellery box stayed firmly shut at the bottom of my wardrobe. I didn't question that my brother, a perfectly healthy nineteen-year-old just dropped dead for no apparent reason.

Maybe that's my problem: I don't question enough.

A couple of times I considered telling our (well, just mine now) parents but the *sensible* part of me said it was childish. How could a jewellery box have anything to do with Alexis dying?

I chose to ignore my suspicions and carry on as normal. Well, as normal as is possible when your brother's just died.

Until the funeral.

It was a sharp, icy morning. I stepped out and the cold air stung my face. The sky was an appropriate morbid grey although it didn't rain. I remember the crunching of my boots on the thin layer of frost in the graveyard, like bones breaking.

manage it. They fell downwards again and I knew that she was sad.

Then she spoke: 'You are the only friend I have ever had and I will always remember you.'

They told her to hurry up, that they had to go. She looked at me again and threw her arms around my neck. I don't know why but it felt nice. Then we broke apart and she was taken away.

I found out that she was imprisoned in a laser cell on the edge of town. I wanted to see her. I couldn't take it anymore. I slipped a laser-resisting device in my pack and headed off. I hadn't a clue where I was going. It was the end of the day before I found her. The windows were blocked by lasers, but I used my device to stop them and I slipped in through the window. I talked to her but she was quiet. I asked her what was wrong and she explained that she was going to be executed. My insides tightened and I didn't know why. I didn't like it. I wanted to save her, but I knew I couldn't. I stayed through the night. Then, when it became too dark, I had to leave. She touched her lips to mine and I returned it. After it, I felt fiery hot. Then I returned home.

Not many people came to see the execution

but I wanted to be with her. She stared right at me with her blue eyes. The executioner was getting ready. She whispered under her breath, 'I love you.' I said it back, not entirely understanding the meaning but doing it all the same. I felt moisture on my face. I reached up to brush away what I now knew were tears. Then it happened. I watched her pale lifeless body being carried away and I felt terrible. I think I understand what loneliness is now.

Many years before this:
The prime minister had never seen anything like it. They looked like apes – though slightly more human in a subtle way. They had come the day before, and called themselves 'sapiens'.

The poor man looked across at the creature sitting opposite him, telling him of a planet far away, of war and destruction. He listened to him explain that the sapiens could advance Earth's technology and benefit the country. He asked for a compromise – he would let a fair portion of their kind live in his country, and both species would abide by each other's laws. He was told that other countries had already allowed them to live there.

This was madness, pure madness, but somehow it sounded fair. He thought to himself, 'Maybe, just maybe, this is the start of something good.'

Granny Ocean

Eleanor Salkeld, age 12,
South Wilts Grammar School, Salisbury

'Why were her toes like that?' I find myself asking.

My mother gives me a sharp look. My grandmother, just returned from Australia, has come to live with us. She lived there for twenty years. I don't really remember her that well. But now my grandmother dominates our spare room. 'They've always been like that,' Mom answers.

Gran arrived just a week ago, and she settled pretty quickly, despite not being in England for an impossibly long time. She's just gone out shopping. Barefoot.

She's a bit weird, my grandmother, I've

always known that. But it was still a shock to see that she goes about barefoot, letting the whole world see that between her toes is an opaque layer of skin. To be honest, there are a lot of weird things about Gran, but I don't want to sit all day talking about how long she likes to loll in the bath (with added salt), how she likes to sit for hours listening to the sound of running water from a tap, or pressing her ear to the inside of a shell, or the fact that fish is her favourite food.

'Having webbed feet is unusual, but it isn't unheard of.' Mom turns away to hide her expression.

'It is, however, unheard of when you go about in town with bare feet,' I argue.

'It's also unheard of to talk about your grandmother in that way.' Mom throws a frosty glare at me over her shoulder, before turning away again.

I pull a face behind her back.

'Anyway,' Mom continues, 'tomorrow Gran says we're going to the beach as a *family*, whether you like it or not.'

I roll my eyes dramatically and leave the room.

Tomorrow. What will it be like? All I know is that she'll do something weird. But I don't know what. In fact, I can't even begin to guess. I've always known that Gran's weird, even though I've only really *personally* known Gran for a week. Mom always used to like rattling on about how strange she is. But now *I* do it, Mom gets angry. Maybe only the son or daughter is allowed to insult their mother. Oh, well. I'll just have to put up with it. And I can only wait...until tomorrow.

We're in the car. Going to the beach. That's Gran in the front, next to Mom in the driver's seat. I'm at the back. Gran looks young, with her ginger-blonde hair, (only a few greys!), and her dark, supple tanned skin. She's fighting fit too. Mom always used to joke that you had to be really fit in Australia so you could get away from all of the hungry crocs. Now, of course, she doesn't.

'It'll be lovely on the beach, as a whole family,' says Mom. She gives me a meaningful look in the rear-view mirror. 'Yes, Charles?'

I'll have to suppress a groan. 'Yes, Mom,' I answer, as sweetly as I can. I don't like the name Charles. I only want to be known as Charlie.

We're arriving. I'm actually quite excited. What weird thing will Gran do? Gran's like some kind of acrobat in a show; you're kind of nervous but you can't wait to see what they'll do next.

Everything seems normal…for now. Mom sets out a picnic rug and lots of food that she prepared yesterday: sandwiches, boiled eggs, crisps, apples and suchlike. Gran just sits there, looking out to sea, a thoughtful look on her face.

'Here we are,' Mom says cheerfully.

We eat.

'The sky's nice today.' Mom tries to make conversation.

'Yes,' Gran agrees, 'but the sea looks even nicer.'

Mom stares. Why? It's a normal comment, but Mom looks horrified.

'Let's swim,' Gran continues. 'Will you join me, Charlie?'

'No,' Mom interrupts firmly. 'Charles will help me clear up.'

I look between the two. What's going on?

'Anyway,' Mom adds, 'it's getting late. Why don't we all go home?'

'But what's wrong with a swim?' I protest,

stubbornly. The two look flustered, almost angry. 'It's not that late. The Sun's barely setting.'

'That's my boy.' Gran grins and runs to the water's edge. I do the same, nervously. Mom's staring at me silently, with a pleading, almost desperate, look on her face. I stare quietly back, daring her to protest. So what's wrong with a swim? Mom worries too much.

Gran and I enter the sea, leaving Mom back at the picnic rug. I pause a moment, partly because the water's cold, partly because I'm remembering how meek, how powerless she looked. I glance at Gran. She's swimming slowly around in a relaxed way, totally oblivious to the cold. She's very good. Like an otter, she's perfectly streamlined, and cuts through the water like a knife through butter. I'll admit, I'm impressed.

Now I realise why. It's her feet – her webbed hands and feet – that are causing her to be like a fish in the sea. She slides gracefully through the water, so quick, so easily…gradually getting further and further away.

'Gran,' I'm calling her. I glance back and I see Mom's waving, calling me.

'Charlie! Charlie, come back.'

I'll pretend I haven't heard. 'GRAN!' I yell. It's no use. She's out of earshot. She dives. I wait. She doesn't come back up. 'GRAN!!!' I scream again. I start swimming forward.

'BOO!!' Gran bursts up through the water, right in front of me. I start, and choke on a lungful of water. It's impossible. She simply *couldn't* have swum all the way back to me in the time she was underwater.

Gran laughs. 'Come with me, Charles.' Suddenly she's serious, holding out her hand. 'Let's go.'

'Go where?' I say stupidly. I'm numb.

'Come on,' she coaxes again.

Suddenly I notice a cut, slicing underneath her ears. No, it's not a cut. It's gills.

'Charlie! *Charlie!*' Mom's screeching out from land, far away.

Gran cocks her head. 'Please,' she says. 'I don't want to go alone.'

There's a splash. Mom's entered the water. Her clothes are still on. 'Charlie,' she yells. She swims frantically towards us, clothes plastered to her skin. 'Get away,' she hisses. 'You can go, but leave Charlie.'

Gran looks at me. I understand now, but at the same time, I don't. 'Charlie?' she says, her voice uncertain...

'I can't go,' I find myself saying.

'But they're coming,' Gran whispers, and suddenly there are many whispering voices, and I see strange faces in the foam, human but not human. Gran stares at me. Then she dives. She's gone, leaving only the sigh of the sea.

'She was always half-half,' Mom tells me later. She doesn't say half what, but then again, I don't need to be told. 'She always wanted to leave.'

'Can we go back though?' I ask. 'Can we see her?'

'We can try,' Mom answers.

We go back. The sea is calm today, tranquil. 'Gran,' I call softly. I won't speak loudly. I know she can hear me. 'Gran. I hope you're OK here... but maybe – maybe we'll see each other again...?'

There is no answer. I don't expect one. All I hear is the sea, sighing.

Quintus was hurrying home from the forum with a basket of stuffed dormice when he came face to face with a boy who could have been his twin.

Caroline Lawrence

Back Through the Book

**Lulu Chrupek, age 12,
Exeter School, Devon**

'*Q*uintus was hurrying home from the
forum with a basket of stuffed dormice
when he came face to face with a boy who
could have been his twin. Translate this sentence
into Latin.' BORING!

Sammy slammed his textbook shut and
sighed. Why was homework always so dull,
he wondered?

Sammy sighed again and stood up. He
announced to the empty study that he needed an
energy boost, before pushing open the heavy oak
door and plodding off to the kitchen.

When Sammy returned clutching a recently
opened packet of jaffa cakes, he was met with

a complication. On every available surface sat Roman senators, all wearing identical white togas and brown leather sandals.

Met with this somewhat unusual sight, Sammy's mouth dropped open, as did the box of jaffa cakes. Disturbed by the sound of chocolate-covered orange jelly and sponge biscuits falling to the floor, the senators ceased their meeting, and turned to face Sammy.

There was silence (all the jaffa cakes were now gathering dust on the polished wooden flooring). Then one of the senators, an older-looking man with tanned skin and blue eyes, started to speak to Sammy. 'Dear stranger,' said the blue-eyed senator, 'we have come to your tablino...'

Another senator with kindly brown eyes nudged him.

'Sorry,' said the blue-eyed senator, 'I mean your *study*, to ask a favour of you. My name is Caius. What is yours? We need you to help us find a missing person. If you succeed, you will be greatly rewarded. Will you help us?'

'My name is Sammy and...erm...' Sammy looked confused. He considered his options. He could say no, or he could say yes. Not much choice then, he thought.

Eventually, after a few rushed moments of quiet consideration, Sammy decided to say yes, because he was just happy that the senators hadn't come to capture him as a slave, and he didn't want to push his luck.

'Thank you very much. We are most, most grateful,' said Caius, who took Sammy's hand and shook it warmly. 'Now come with us, and we can brief you on your mission.'

Sammy removed his hand from Caius' grip, then asked, 'Erm, where exactly are you taking me?'

Caius smiled, 'Why, we're going back through the book.'

Before Sammy had time to ask any more questions (he had many), Caius gripped his arm and led him to the beech desk where Sammy's textbook lay shut. Caius opened it and flicked to page 91, where Sammy saw the exercise about Quintus he had got stuck on. Sammy followed Caius onto the desk and stood beside him.

'When I say 'GO', jump into the book,' Caius explained. 'When you are thr...'

'But Caius, that's a school textbook; I can't just go jumping on it,' Sammy argued.

Caius ignored him. '...When you are through, hold on to my arm at all times. Simple, yes? Well then. Ready, set, GO!'

Caius jumped, and Sammy went with him, his eyes firmly shut. Instead of immediately landing on the book and rendering it forever crumpled, they seemed to be falling forever. Sammy nervously opened his eyes.

He was surrounded by blue, thousands of different hues of it, all blended together due to the speed at which they were falling. Sammy looked up, and saw more senators following them. Sammy guessed that they were in a never-ending tunnel.

He was half right. It was definitely a tunnel, but it came to an abrupt end when they hit a cold, hard, marble floor. Caius and the rest of the senators landed softly on their feet. Sammy, however, not being used to this unusual way of travelling, landed hard on his rear.

'Welcome to the Temple of Mars.' Caius introduced Sammy to their whereabouts.

'Erm,' mumbled Sammy, 'can I ask you a

few questions?'

'Certainly, Sammy,' replied Caius.

'Well, how come you can speak English?' Sammy began. 'Where are we? Who am I supposed to be finding? When did he disappear? What was he doing? Where was he seen last?'

'Slow down there,' Caius defended himself against any more questions. 'Here goes...We can speak English because of where we live. You're bound to learn it, if you live in an English to Latin textbook.'

Sammy just stood there, his mouth hanging open (again).

'As for the person you're going to find,' continued Caius, 'well, his name is Quintus. And this is what witnesses say: 'Quintus was hurrying home from the forum with a basket of stuffed dormice when he came face to face with a boy who could have been his twin.' They also say that the boy who could have been his twin invited him to his house for dinner. This was two weeks ago. Quintus hasn't been seen since.'

'But that thing about Quintus hurrying home from the forum,' Sammy said unbelievingly, 'is just an exercise from my

Latin textbook. It's not real.'

'We live in the textbook, Sammy,' said Caius darkly. 'What you may think is just a story really happens to us.'

Sammy still wasn't fully convinced, but he decided to go along with it. Suddenly a thought struck him. 'So, will I have to do this all by myself? I'm only twelve you know.'

'Don't worry; Petrus here will be with you at all times.' Caius gestured towards the senator with kindly, brown eyes, who stepped forward. 'Now, my fellow senators and I have to be somewhere. When you have found Quintus, I trust you will come and find me?'

And with that, Caius led the rest of the senators (save Petrus) through a door in the far marble wall.

Sammy looked up at Petrus. Petrus was already looking at him. Sammy met Petrus' hazel eyes smiling down at him, and took an immediate liking to him.

Sammy suddenly realised that he must look very strange in his grey hooded top and jeans, as Petrus pointed out to him. 'I'm sure your clothes are very fashionable where you live,' said Petrus, kindly, 'but I don't think people will trust you if you are dressed like that around here. Follow me, and we'll find you some robes.'

When Sammy emerged from the great marble building, wearing a toga, he was greeted by glorious sunshine beaming down at him. He observed his surroundings. He appeared to be in some sort of square. People wearing togas were bustling around, buying goods from market stalls. This must be the forum, Sammy thought. He suddenly thought that it would be nice to maybe take home some stuffed dormice to eat with his parents, so he asked Petrus, who had just emerged out of the marble building behind him, if he could go and get some.

'Yes, but be quick,' Petrus replied in answer to Sammy's question. 'I'll wait here for you.'

Sammy ran around the forum until he found a stall selling stuffed dormice. He paid for a few with some money which Petrus had lent him, said thank you, and left the stall. As he was hurrying back to the marble house with his basket of stuffed dormice, Sammy came face to face with a boy who could have been his twin...

THE TROUBLE WITH HAVING A DOUBLE

Maya Briglia, age 11,
Awliscombe C of E Primary School, Devon

CHAPTER 1
QUINTUS' STORY

Quintus was hurrying home from the forum with a basket of stuffed dormice when he bumped into a boy who could have been his twin. They stared at each other, two pairs of dark-brown eyes transfixed on each other. 'Hello,' said the other boy in a deep voice. 'My name is Marcus.'

'And mine Quintus,' said Quintus.

'So where are you off to?' asked Marcus.

'Home,' said Quintus simply.

'Where do you live?' asked the other.

'Number IX,' said Quintus pointing to a small run-down house with just one window and red crumbling bricks. 'You?'

Marcus pointed, and with a gasp Quintus looked up to see the biggest house he had seen in all the XI years of his life. 'You live there?!!' said Quintus.

'Marcus, where are you?' came a shrill girlie voice. In the blink of an eye Marcus was gone and so was the basket of mice Quintus had been carrying. Suddenly an arm was flung around Quintus' neck and the shrill voice was saying, 'Marcus, I have been so worried about you.' She now let go of Quintus, who turned his now purple face around to look at the large woman with big, baby-blue eyes and three wobbling chins.

V minutes later Quintus found himself stepping out of a chariot and onto the marble steps leading to the great white house.

That night for Quintus was great fun and completely different to anything he had ever experienced before. He had the best bath of his life; it was a giant tiled tub with lavender-scented, hot spring water. After that he got dressed into a fine red and white tunic, the maid came to call him down for the banquet, he ate so many different foods that he had never tasted in his life and drank drinks other than the water that he was used to.

A few weeks later when he had almost completely forgotten who he had been and that this was not his real life, the large lady who he now knew as Miriam took him into town. While she looked at the fine dresses Quintus wandered off.

CHAPTER 2
MARCUS' STORY

Marcus was hurrying to the forum, when he bumped into a boy that could have been his twin. They stared at each other, two pairs of dark-brown eyes transfixed on each other. 'Hello,' said Marcus. 'My name is Marcus.'

'And mine Quintus,' said the other boy.

'So where are you off to?' asked Marcus.

'Home,' said Quintus simply.

'Where do you live?' asked the other.

'Number IX,' said Quintus, pointing to a small, run-down house with just one window and red crumbling bricks. 'You?'

Marcus pointed, and with a gasp Quintus looked up to see the biggest house he had seen in all the XI years of his life. 'You live there?!!' said Quintus.

Suddenly Marcus heard Miriam's voice saying, 'Marcus, where are you?' Then without thinking he grabbed the basket of dormice and ran off. Marcus hid behind a few houses, watching as Quintus walked away to the chariot with Miriam's arms wrapped around him. Marcus thought to himself as he walked over to number IX how boring life had been in his large house on the hill, how routine it had been and how everything was done for him.

When he entered number IX the woman inside, who was dressed in shabby black clothes, turned around and said, 'Where have you been, Quintus? It should have only taken you an hour to do all those chores.' The woman grabbed the basket of stuffed dormice and pushed him back out of the door, telling him to go and fetch some water from the well and then go to chop some firewood before he could even think about having supper.

When eventually he got back to the house

he found there was a man sitting at the old table eating with the woman in black. At first Marcus thought this could have been Quintus' father, but it soon turned out he was a moneylender and she owed him money. Guessing he would not be getting any supper, Marcus found something that looked like a bed, fell onto it, and curled up and fell asleep almost immediately after his hard day's work.

A few weeks later, when he had almost completely forgotten who he had been and that this was not his real life, Marcus was sent on an errand by the woman in black. As he was hurrying home after completing the errand with a basket full of stuffed dormice that he had been told to buy, he bumped into a boy that could have been his twin…!!

Doodles &
ideas

for more stories

Illustrations by: Owen Klemmer-Luck, age 9, Yattendon School, Lauren Mackenzie, age 7, Saul Barry, age 6, SEEDS Home Ed Group

Secret Notes